A WOMAN'S BURDEN

PUBLICATIONS

TABLE OF CONTENTS

—— BIRTH PAINS ——

They lie in the dark confines of the
womb
Two kernels in a warm, moist tomb
Ten little fingers and ten little toes
Fold in as pain begins in her throes

Head down, they slide as they engage
Bloody tissues grind as they disengage
In exultant pain they wait suffused
For passage through a tunnel effaced

For this is joy and sadness too
Here's double for your trouble they coo
She bears down against agonizing pain

Struggling to think only of the gain
For this womb with two was a grave for
one
Having joy, true, yet deeply forlorn
Will these two now in play
Replace the one who did not stay?

— FATE OF A WOMAN —

The wind was strong enough to reverse a chicken's feathers. The first rain of the year hovered just above the pregnant grey clouds whose bellies almost rested on the tallest of the oil palms. Dust and sand carried in the fierce gusts whipped Nkwonma's face, and she pulled off her head tie to use in shielding her nose. Then the rain drops fell. They lashed the earth with venom as if still annoyed over a previous quarrel.

Odinkenmelu saw her pass. Her heart filled with pity, she watched her bend and dash into the village primary school through its low doorway. Then she turned away to lift her fat baby, Nnaa, and wipe his nose. He had been grizzling all day. She felt his forehead, it was still slightly warm. He would need another dose of *ogwu iba* which he hated, before too long. She put him to the breast and reflected on life.

She thought about the plight of a childless woman in a community where children were pure gold. She thought about the day she herself had forced Nnaa out of her womb, crouching on the birth stool and bearing down with all her strength. The wavering cry of her firstborn son. The satisfaction of realizing that her two feet had touched the ground in her husband's homestead. That no one could talk to her anyhow after this.

Her mother had laid the new born infant on her own shrivelled chest, and lifted her eyes brimming with tears to *Chukwu n'enye nwa* in thanksgiving. She herself had been twelve years in her husband's home without children, and as a result, she had two co-wives, Mama Obele and Mama Nke Nta.

Odinkenmelu reflected on Nkwonma's plight. Her heart brimmed with the pity and fellow feeling that only someone who has travelled a rough, stony road feels toward another who must walk the same stretch of road.

Nkwonma hugged her arms around her body in the darkened confines of the primary school's lone building. The east end of the school had lost its roof to the intense wind and its tattered remnants made a sad metallic flapping noise that formed a background to her thoughts. She gathered her wrapper and tucked it between her thighs. Some years ago, she had been a pupil here.

She stared around her at the familiar environment. She thought to herself that even the stinging lashes of Teacher Njoku's cane were better than what she found herself inside now. At least, the pain from the strokes of cane never lasted until recess.

Her mind wandered back to the conversation she had overheard some years ago. The beginning of everything.

"Mama Nma, biakene li." Her parents and most other people called her Nma. They said it suited her best, because even as a baby she had been beautiful.

She wondered why her father was calling for her mother in the thick of preparing the evening meal. He usually let them be at that time because as he jovially said, it made the food arrive faster. Nma was grinding the pepper for the yam pottage they would eat that night, but she suspended her grinding and crept closer to listen when she heard her name, and her mother's shout of "*Chim o!*"

Her younger brother, Chukelu, came over and squatted beside her. She warned him off with a venomous stare and he wandered away grumbling beneath his breath. Nkwonma listened intently.

"Woman, why are you shouting? How old were you when I married you?"

"I was older than Nkwonma, and I was not in school. I want my daughter to finish school."

"Shut up woman!" Through the loud beating of her heart, Nma heard her normally mild mannered father bark at her mother. Then his voice relaxed a little as he searched for humour, "If you did not want your daughter to marry young, why did you produce one so beautiful? Like yourself?" Now, he sounded teasing and sly.

Nma had heard enough. She tightened her wrapper on her waist and walked into the screen of trees behind the house. Thirty minutes or so later she heard her mother shouting,

"Nma! Nkwonma!!" She refused to answer.

The rain was ending. She would soon have to go home. It had only been a cloudburst not deep rain. The fury of the wind had driven most of the rain into the neighboring community, she was certain. She rubbed her hands together. Dry and rough from wielding a hoe to prepare the soil for the year's farming season. She preferred to be in the farm anyway. It was better than being at home.

As she passed with her hoe, Odinkenmelu called out "Nkwo, I saw you run into the school. How far with your ridges on the farm?"

Nma smiled at Odinkenmelu. She was one of the few people who called her Nkwo. Most people, like her parents, called her Nma. The smile lit up her face and Odinkenmelu thought to herself that this girl had to be the prettiest in the entire village. Dark skinned, tall and slim with dimples in both cheeks; even with everything she had been through, she still shone like *ola edo* - pure gold. She reflected ruefully that but for this beauty, Nma might still have been in school. Ardent suitors had begun to come too early, ranging from around the five villages close by. Her father had decided to accept one quickly before anything went wrong with his precious daughter.

The two women exchanged pleasantries and Nkwonma went on into the gathering dusk, dragging her feet, taking more time than the few minutes' walk on the bush path connecting the two homesteads warranted.

Emeka was drinking palm wine alone inside his obi as she arrived. She greeted him, but there was no answer. He only turned blood stained corneas in her direction. She passed on quickly; now hurrying to get to the kitchen. She knew that the storm ahead would put the one that had just passed overhead to shame.

The first blow landed on her back as she bent to push a piece of firewood deeper into the fire she was trying to build to boil yam for the evening meal. She arched her back in pain as wafts of alcohol wrapped around her face.

"Where are you coming from eh? Where are you coming from you harlot?" Each bellow was accompanied by a burning slap. Nma felt herself falling, felt the shocking sting as her hand encountered the cooking fire, then she was running, wailing, blindly twisting and turning as if to evade a pursuer, but he had not followed her.

Through the raging fever that had descended on her, Nma heard her mother's voice in the next room. Her hand and her head throbbed to the rhythm of the same unseen drums.

"*Papa Nma, ike agwugo m*. I am tired. Is this how to marry a wife? If we let this girl go back to this man, he will kill her. Is she *Chineke n'akpu nwa?* Is it her fault that she has not had children?" She hissed, a long drawn out sound filled with pain.

There was no reply from her father. She imagined him biting his lower lip and shaking his legs as he did when perturbed. She wished Chukelu was here. He would have been a good distraction from this inner and outer pain, but he had gone to Nnewi to be apprenticed to a big time trader there. The house was very quiet without him and full of thoughts. Not for the first time, she wondered why her parents had only two children. It was unusual in this community. Here children were priceless. Nma was sure there had to be a story behind it, but whenever she asked, Mama, she would only say,

"Someday I will tell you my story." Someday never seemed to come.

There was a knock on the wooden door of her room, and Nkwonma wondered who it could be. She kept few friends, even her childhood friends, because she had no energy for gossip.

"Can I come in?" It was Odinkenmelu's voice.

Nma cheered up immediately. She liked the older woman.

Odinkenmelu came in with her baby perched on her hip. Nma wished she could reach for the fat little child and hold him. She loved children, but the pain in her hand felt like the throbbing from a big boil waiting to be lanced.

"*Nne m kedu?* How are you?" Odii's face was full of concern. I heard you shouting the other day, but I had no one to leave this boy with and moreover, he was feverish. What is it?"

The two women chatted for a while, and on her way out, Odinkenmelu turned once more to look at Nma. The visit was all too brief. The older woman had to hurry home to cook supper.

"That man will never change. Leave him. If your mother had not left her first husband to marry your father she would no longer be alive. Why can't she ask you to do what she did to save your life?"

She said nothing further, but quietly went out and shut the door behind her. Nma could hear Odii wishing her parents a safe night as she left.

So that was the answer to the mystery? Her father was not her mother's first husband then. She had been married before. For how long? Nma wondered. Did she have step brothers and sisters? What had made Mama to run away from her first marriage? Odinkenmelu had hinted that her first husband had been violent like Emeka. Did this fate then run in families? Nkwonma bit her lip and swallowed a sob. How could she leave Emeka? It would be a big disgrace. Women in her family line did not leave their homes. But apparently, her mother had left hers to survive. Why had Mama hidden this story from her? How come Odinkenmelu knew and she did not?

"Odinkenmelu was one of the teenage girls who saw me run into this village from the next one, almost naked, the day I came home. They were coming back from the stream. She knows everything about it." Mama shook her head as the dark memories flooded back in. "Igwulube told me he would feed me the poison he uses for catching fish if I continued to stay. He beat me, and nearly stripped me naked the day I finally decided to leave."

"Why?" Nma stared at her mother's face.

"We had been married six years, and I had no child."

Nma spliced the fingers of both hands together and rested her chin on them.

"Mama I will not go back to Emeka."

"My daughter do not say that. Where will you stay? Your father will not let you back into this house."

"Then I will jump into Otamiri River."

Emeka arrived after two weeks. Nma cynically reflected that he was probably tired of cooking his own food and sweeping the compound; that is if he had not found some other woman to do it for him. He came smelling of arrogance and self-assurance. Had he not paid the bride price on her head?

Until that money was returned, she remained his wife.

She meekly followed him home, but deep in her heart she knew it would not be for too long.

"*Nne m imakazi!*" Nma turned to see Ulunne, one of her classmates from her days in the village school. Ulunne was short and broad with a dazzling smile. She was preparing for her wedding after the year's rains, and was on her way to Eke market to buy some things.

Nma smiled, "it is God o!" She was used to compliments on all sides these days. Her pregnancy suited her, and she knew everyone in the village was happy for her. Who did not know what she had gone through in the name of looking for a child?

The two young women exchanged a few more pleasantries, and Nkwonma went on. She was going from there to Ofia Enwe to get some *utazi* leaves to make pepper soup. She found herself craving savoury hot dishes like never before, with a tinge of bitter to them, thus the *utazi*. From there, she would go to see Odinkenmelu. She hoped that by the time she got home, Emeka would not have returned from Ebeagu where he had gone to trade.

She touched her swollen tummy. She was six months pregnant, getting to the time she would see her beautiful daughter. She knew that what was inside her body was a girl, and she found herself praying to *Chukwu bi n'igwe* that this child would escape the fate she and her own mother had endured at the hands of life.

As she returned in the early evening, she saw that Emeka was already back. His Raleigh bicycle leaned on the mud wall of the obi. He dashed out immediately he saw her. "Where are you coming from? Village prostitute! So even with a big stomach you cannot sit still?" Before she could say a word, he ran back into the obi and emerged with a sharpened machete that he used for cutting palm fruits.

Nkwonma forgot that she was pregnant and ran like an antelope pursued by a lion. She ran in the direction of the river. She could hear Emeka's feet pounding behind her, but after a while, she heard nothing more. Then she threw herself on the ground, and wept from deep inside her womb, great wracking sobs that tore her savagely from within. When she got up, she knew she would not return.

The villagers scoured the banks of the mighty Otamiri River looking for Nma's bloated corpse. They found nothing. They refused to give up, going as far as the Niger whose tributary Otamiri was. They still saw nothing.

For three days, they went and returned, bone tired. The girl seemed to have vanished from the earth. Where could a six month pregnant woman have wandered to? They went foot by foot through the rain forest near the river, and still, there was nothing.

Emeka said, "Maybe the *Mammy Water* in the river has claimed her own. I have always said that the girl I married is not an ordinary person." He folded his arms into his armpits and shook his head in bewilderment. Villagers cursed him quietly behind his back.

Mama Nma wept as if her heart would break like a clay water pot, until four days after her daughter's disappearance.

Chukelu, who had returned at the bad news of his sister's disappearance, saw Odinkenmelu enter his mother's room on the fourth day. He heard the two women whispering together. He saw his mother emerge from her room wiping her eyes with the corner of her wrapper. After that, she wept no more.

——— TERROR!! ———

Maimuna Mainasara shivered. From the back of the mud granary close to the wall, she peeped out again, and just then, a flash of light painted the wall near where she was hidden. She made herself very small and shrank back into the darkness. Heart beating very fast, she sat back on her haunches, closed her eyes and tried to imagine that she was still asleep and that this was a dream.

The men had come while the village slept. That night, a fading moon bathed the huts in a tired glow that barely disturbed the darkness. Maimuna slept in her mother's hut with Mairo and Amina, her two younger sisters. Her brothers who were all older slumbered peacefully in another hut nearby. Seven year old Mairo and six year old Amina slept, limbs tangled together, on a separate mat from Maimuna's. Muna, as her mother called her, lay on one mat alone to avoid the two younger girls kicking her like donkeys all night long.

Maybe it was Amina talking in her sleep that woke her up; maybe it was one of the skinny village dogs that suddenly started barking with its whole body, but Maimuna came awake with a jerk and saw a shadow pass the open window. It was the shadow of a man. Her blood creeping through her veins, she crawled over to her mother, "Uwa, uwa," she shook her gently. Her mother murmured something and turned over.

C- r- a- s- h! The wooden door of the hut splintered, and a man jumped in. He was dressed in army uniform with a shawl wrapped round his head. He held a gun in one hand, and a flashlight in the other. He reached down, pulled up Maimuna's mother who was still dazed from being suddenly woken, slinging his gun on his shoulder to do so, and roughly pushed her out through the door.

Maimuna did not think twice. At thirteen, she knew she would be next, but they had no use for little ones like Mairo and Amina. The two small children would be safe even if badly frightened. She jumped through the window and ran hunched over toward the granary, dodging fleeing villagers. Dogs barked, the invaders shouted and threatened, hit men and women with the butts of their guns, pushed and pulled others toward waiting vehicles.

Thinking quickly now, Maimuna slunk out from behind the granary and started dodging between the huts toward the entrance of the village. She had thought of hiding inside the mud silo, but soon decided they might burn the village, and she would roast there like a rat caught in a bush fire.

Midway, she felt a hand grab her arm and she looked up at one of the night attackers. There was no face to see. It was hidden in the folds of his shawl. Only a pair of burning eyes that even the weak moonlight could not hide glared down at her. Maimuna stifled her scream of J – e – e – s – u – s!

and tried to jerk free. The nightmare tightened his grip.

Heart pounding, the young girl joined other people at the vehicles. They all looked dazed and terrified. Quickly, the invaders sorted out the villagers into men and boys, women, and young girls. Maimuna stood beside Tamira, her friend. Tamira was shaking with fear and Maimuna whispered to her. "Be strong. God is with us."

"If you are a Christian, step this way. Others stay where you are," one of the men hissed at them.

Without hesitation, Maimuna stepped forward. She looked at

Tamira. Her friend looked away and bowed her head.

As they drove away, Maimuna thought she saw her mother being forced unto another vehicle. It was too dark to be sure. She bowed her head and prayed like she had never prayed before in her life; that she would live, and that someday, she would be re-united with her family. She thought of little Mairo and Amina all alone and frightened, and she nearly started crying, but just then, it was as if she heard the voice of Mr. Theophilus Wamba, the missionary who had brought Christ to her village five years ago, say, "Peace, my child, He will never leave you nor forsake you."

After her father died, Mr. Wamba had become something of a replacement for Maimuna and her brothers and sisters. He taught them about Jesus, led them to faith and trained them in the Bible. Uwa was the last to believe, and Maimuna remembered the joy of that day when the entire circle of her family stood complete in Christ.

Two years ago, Bro. Theophilus had been posted to another field and replaced by one of the native deacons, Yakubu Wuya. She would always miss him. She wished he were here now to strengthen her, but on second thoughts she thanked God that he was not. He would have been killed immediately.

"Shh," a strong hand clamped down on her mouth and Maimuna tried to wriggle free. She glared at the owner of the hand.

"Shhh. I am your friend. I will not hurt you. Just listen to me."

Maimuna nodded, and the young soldier removed his hand and sat down beside her. He spoke in a low voice. "I want to help you get away from here, but it will not be easy."

"Why?" whispered Maimuna, "why would you want to help me? Are you not afraid they will kill you?"

"No. I too have become a Christian. When I said, 'If you are a Christian, step this way. Others stay where you are,' I was surprised to see you come forward immediately. That picture refused to leave my head. I too was kidnapped from my village two years ago and forced to join these people. My people worship Dodo. We have heard of Jesus, but we didn't know what to make of the message. When you stepped forward, I said surely, there must be something in this thing to make a small girl like this to risk death. I remembered the things missionaries who came to my village told us, and I prayed the prayer to God."

Maimuna bowed her head, her heart jumping with praise to God. Could it be that God had sent her to this young man as a witness? She remembered Paul locked in a jail at Philippi, being used to save the jailer and his family.

They trekked for three days to the village of Pambunga. Sometimes, the young soldier carried Muna on his back because her feet were cracked and bleeding. Several times, they came across dangerous snakes. Once, they had to cross a river. Fortunately in this dry season, it was shallow and they got across safely. Sule dug roots for them to eat, and picked fruits from the trees. After two years, he knew his way around these forests very well and so they arrived at Pambunga on the third day as dusk gathered.

The village swarmed with internally displaced persons, and almost immediately, Maimuna's prayers were answered. She saw her mother sitting under a tree near a cooking fire. Screaming with joy, Muna ran into her mother's arms. Uwa embraced her daughter with tears streaming down her face.

"What of my brothers? What of Mairo and Amina?"

"We are all safe. We have lost everything, but we have our lives. God be praised."

"How did it happen?"

"Soldiers came soon after they took you away and fought with the invaders. Almost everyone was rescued."

"What of Tamira and the other girls who said they were not Christians?"

"They drove away with those ones also. We found them later. They are all dead."

Maimuna remembered a verse from the Bible, *"For whosoever will save his life shall lose it: but whosoever will lose his life for my sake, the same shall save it."*

She bowed her head and wept.

—— **FIRST LADY** ——

You couldn't really rely on these men of God. Her lips twisted bitterly, she realized that he would still be there to pray for the next one and the next until all things had passed away – regardless of their ideological persuasions.

Cynthia Manuel-Giwa paused for one moment to admire her image in the hall mirror. She looked around her with satisfaction. Who would ever have thought that she, Cynthia Maku, would someday sit as the brightest jewel in the glittering tiara that was State House, No. 1 Jacaranda Avenue, Ajabu? She adjusted the real-life diamonds on her fleshy neck, brushed back a wisp of relaxed hair tickling her forehead and prepared to descend into the swirl of humanity that had gathered for Independence Day Celebrations in the brightly lit Main Hall.

Sycophant, she thought to herself as the Minister for Information rushed to her side at the foot of the grand staircase. A medium sized man with skin that glowed like polished mahogany, he was one of the worst.

Outside, she smiled and acknowledged the exaggerated compliment he paid her. Others crowded round. The power behind the throne. She shook hands graciously, bowed, smiled, but nothing went past the surface. Her heart was turning to cold grey stone. Had already turned to a lump of flint?

She watched Ebenezer Manuel-Giwa greet a young woman in a décolleté ice blue gown in the French manner – one kiss to either cheek. He had studied in France, and affected these continental mannerisms. She looked at him with dissatisfaction, her husband, President and Commander-in-Chief of the republic. Jealousy curled like a green serpent in her heart. She knew she had seen that girl before. Was she not one of his many secret diversions? Inside, she hissed, outside she smiled and walked over to stand beside him. She would preside over this semi-formal and "intimate" dinner for perhaps three hundred of the worst, but she would not enjoy it. Today was her forty ninth birthday and Independence Day.

With the Minister for Power and Steel jabbering something in her ear to her right, she allowed her mind to drift.

Yesterday, Rev. (Dr.) Joseph Amboni, General Overseer, Light of the World Ministries, had been in State House to pray for her on the eve of her birthday and to commit the nation to God on its fortieth. As always, his prayers were vaulting and colourful. She had to restrain herself from asking him, "Is it true that you support the Vice President's presidential ambitions?"

Since the day he had predicted that Manuel-Giwa would win the 2004 Presidential elections with a 2/3 majority and it had come to pass, he had become a State House favourite. Some of his other predictions had come true as well, and she found herself developing a healthy respect for his powers as a prophet.

Abruptly, she asked him, "How come you have never tried to preach to me, to convert me?"

The Man of God looked shocked. "But you are a Christian?"

"Do you hear the things they say about me out there? Do you read the newspapers? Do you realize that they say I am the power behind the throne and that this is the worst and most corrupt government this country has ever had? What do you think the future holds, sir?"

Shock, confusion and embarrassment chased themselves across the reverend's face. He stammered,

"Madam, you cannot listen to what everyone says. These are disgruntled elements who never see anything good in any administration. 2008 is certain by divine revelation."

She smiled, reached across a thick envelope to him "for his journey back" and thanked him for the prayers and best wishes.

When the first explosion took place, jerking every head in the hall toward the State House entrance, blood cold in Cynthia's veins, she had just enough thought left to reflect that yes, it was a terrible mistake to trust these Men of God and their prophecies.

—— **THIRD PARTY** ——

This institution is not for suppression
It is not meant to be a condition
Bringing on desperate supplication

But when reality dawns,
I look around upon
a space just big enough for two

And I ask...
How did it come to encompass you
too?

— THE PRICE WAS BLOOD —

Nwando made rippling tapping motions with her manicured nails on the wooden arm of her chair, then brought herself up short. Nasty habit. She sighed mentally. Any time she was stressed, she tapped the arm of whatever she was sitting on. She shifted slightly, pulling her blouse forward and blowing into her cleavage. This heat topped everything. She was already feeling pregnant.

Her mind wandered over the events of yesterday; picking up each image, staring at it closely, and dropping it into a basket in her mind. First up, Aunty Makuo's phone call which was epic as usual:

"Hello, is that our wife?" Voice thick with sarcasm. Her husband's step sister's voice always wore a thick coat of sarcasm for whatever strange reason. "Please prepare the guest room for me. Put that my favourite bedsheet o; I should be with you people by next week; I have a conference in Abuja."

Just like that.

Nwando's mind faded back to the last visit. It was a year ago, they had been married three years and were moving house. Packages and boxes formed a small angular hill in the corner of the living room under dust sheets, the furniture was due to be moved out that day. That's when the phone rang. Nwando thought of letting it ring out, but then she took the call and immediately wished she hadn't.

She remembered that Obiora had been determined she would meet all his close family before the traditional wedding. Fortunately, most of them lived in Enugu, so hopping from house to house wouldn't be too much of a problem. Nwando felt so excited. Mama and Papa had proved to be lovely people, and she hoped everyone else would be too. She twisted her long natural hair into a topknot, put on a fitted green skirt, a loose cream top with a Peter Pan collar – demure without being sanctimonious - and flicked on some basic make up. Obiora told her "you spin my world" like he always did when she put in some extra effort for him. She felt good, and she knew she looked good.

Aunty Makuo's house was in a block of four luxury flats, up two flights of steps. Before they could knock on the door, a large, dark woman with a carefully made up face pulled the door open and said without a smile,

"Obiora, you're late. I told you to bring her by 2pm, I have a meeting in church by 4:30pm. We have exactly one hour."

They trailed her into a living room that looked as if it had stepped off the pages of a Home and Garden magazine. Nwando looked around her in some awe wondering where it would be alright to sit. The place didn't look as if it had ever been used before. Obiora's sister commanded them to sit down, and they dropped into the nearest white couch. She stared at Nwando for what felt like five minutes but was probably much less, and asked Obiora,

"This is the girl?"

Obiora said, "Makuo, she's Nwando, the girl I want to marry."

"Are you Scripture Union? Why do you have natural hair?" Nwando wondered if she had just heard correctly. She found herself blinking stupidly, wondering where to start answering such a question.

"And she is so tiny, like a shrimp, do you eat at all? Or are you one of those girls that pretend they don't like food because they can't cook?"

Nwando felt her inner person coming to a boil, and she stared at

Makuo trying to keep the dislike out of her face, fighting for a small smile.

Obiora jumped in with, "Of course, she can cook," and Nwando felt the fires inside raging hotter. Your sister insults me the first time she meets me, and that is all you can say?

She beat a rapid tattoo on the armrest of the settee and caught herself just in time. This woman was a predator. You don't show predators you are nervous. She folded her hands in her lap and thought to herself, "*Nwando, you don enter.*"

Nwando saw again in her mind's eye, her sister-in-law walking confidently into the littered space that was their living room, and asking, "And what is all this?" At the same time, confidently pushing her carry-on luggage toward the younger woman with her toe. She obviously expected Nwando to relieve her of it and bear it like a slave into the guest room.

"Aunty, you remember I told you we are moving house?" Nwando knew she sounded tart, but she couldn't help it.

Obiora's sister eyed her with corresponding acidity, "You don't have to be sarcastic, please. I know I am menopausal, but I am not stupid. I remember you told me that you're moving on the phone. Please if it is not convenient for you, I can always stay in a hotel."

That's when her husband came downstairs, took the cabin luggage upstairs, "Makuo, how can we be in Abuja and you will be staying in a hotel?" Nwando remembered eyeing his back as he went up the stairs with his sister in tow. She turned away wondering what the next couple of days would be like.

She fanned herself with her hand, dragging again at her damp blouse. The next couple of days had been bad to put it mildly. Most of it was Makuo complaining about one thing or the other. The soup was too salty. The air conditioner in the room was not cooling the way she wanted it. Her bath water was lukewarm. Nwando felt she could have tolerated the woman's excesses for Obiora's sake if not for the part about, "How come you people have been married three years, and there is nothing to show for it?"

"Can you talk to your sister?" She leaned on the door of their bedroom, the only place she felt safe during this visit and looked pleadingly at Obiora.

"It's not that I don't know what to tell her, it's just that I respect you. Please tell her it's no business of hers whether I am pregnant or not, why and why not…"

Obiora looked at her with some dislike, "Madam, she is only here for a couple of days. Can you try and tolerate her that long? After all she's my sister. Think about it; I don't bother about what your people do or don't do when they come here."

It took Nwando a full minute to shut her mouth that had swung open like a door in the wind. All she could see was the brown grains on the wooden door he had shut in her face.

Nwando stood up and walked around desultorily. She noted that the golden palm needed water. And right there in the centre of the living room ceiling was a cobweb shadowed with dust joining one of the glass bits on the chandelier to the other. Nwando hated cobwebs and the spiders that made them. She trailed her hand along the dresser, there was dust too. Everywhere was dusty.

She felt hot, lethargic and even a little faint. She picked up another image from yesterday, dropped it into her tidy-mind basket and hoped it would stay there. Yesterday, she had been in to see her gynaecologist and he had told her she would need a cervical cerclage or a bedrest or both.

Nwando wondered why this pregnancy now that it was here had refused to let her live a semblance of a normal life. The worst part of it all was that Obiora, her darling husband, was as useless as a left hand when it came to house chores. She had barely stopped herself from vomitting into the food he had wrestled up the other day when she was running a low grade temperature. And now this woman was on her way here again. Who would do all the catering and waitressing?

She thought about Makuo for the umpteenth time that day. She enjoyed calling her Makuo in her head; it was her little piece of rebellion. The woman wasn't her aunt for God's sake, although she was much older. Sometimes, she felt sorry for her. Her husband had vamoosed five years ago with a younger woman, leaving her with two girls studying abroad to cater for. According to Obiora, the man said he had *"dashed"* her the girls.

Sometimes, she didn't blame this husband she had never met, sometimes she did. As far as she was concerned, he had a lot to do with the negative force called Makuo traipsing all over the landscape withering everything in its path. She thought about Obiora telling her his step sister had paid his way through the last two years of university because Papa had a financial meltdown of sorts as he came out of his second year. Not for the first time, Nwando wondered how long it would be, if ever, before this debt of gratitude was paid in full.

She smiled wryly as she realized she woke up every day thanking God that there was only one Makuo. Her husband's family were delicious people. Sweet and simple, and anyway, most of his own full siblings had found their way abroad at some point or the other. Only one other one was in Nigeria and Okey was just great. They had seen him in Enugu as well on that visit.

Up in the guest room, Nwando could hear the murmur of conversation blending with the sound of the television from downstairs. The mattress in the guestroom upstairs was heavy, and Nwando tried to lift it using only her shoulders, but suddenly, she felt a stitch and a warm gush of blood. Her mind went dark. She was losing the baby. She held her lower belly foolishly, helplessly just standing there, feeling the warm liquid trickling down her legs. She must have shouted without realizing it, because running footsteps came up the stairs, and Obiora was at the door with Makuo peeping in from behind him.

"Nwando, are you crazy?" He was screaming. She seemed to hear him from a distance as if she was detached from her ears. "Why are you making the bed again? You made that damned bed this morning."

Nwando clutched her tummy, "Aunty said she would still like her favourite bedsheet, I forgot she told me last week…"

He lifted her effortlessly, turned to his sister, roared, "Are you satisfied now? I will take you to the airport or to the hotel whenever I get back, whichever you want, and don't come back here ever again until I say so."

As he walked carefully down the stairs, trying not to bump her, Nwando felt the dark red blood leaking out of her. She thought slowly, painfully, so the price was always going to be my blood?

— A MOTHER'S PRAYER —

"Areeaaaa!"

Dibiuno, Dibi, for short, pushed his face cap slightly more askew. He added a mild limp to his swagger. A clenched fist salute assured Scarface that he had been noticed. Dibi was on one last sweep of his territory before he retired for the night. Disgusted, he scraped off some stuff from his boot unto the crumbling edge of a broken down wall bordering the dark street. A revolting smell drifted up to his flared nostrils. Dog shit! He swore under his breath and imagined cutting the throats of the stinking stray dogs that littered this neighbourhood one after the other.

He turned unto Makalele Street and folded himself into a dark doorway as a police vehicle with wailing siren throttled past.

"Animals!" he cursed.

Their patrols had become more regular since Ironbar was killed behind Metro Cinema two weeks ago. Finally, he turned the corner into Freebay Close. He sat down on the back stairs of his parents' house, No. 16, and listened to his father, Pastor Silas Orasi, leading family prayer. He smiled slightly as he mouthed the words of the song they were singing inside the darkened house: *Jesus loves me this I know, for the Bible tells me so...* He thought he could detect a break in his father's voice as he sang the song. He sat very still on the top step. He would not go in just yet. Not until everyone was asleep. He could not bear the thought of his mother's sobbing and whining. Not tonight. He might be tempted to do something violent to her.

To pass the time, he searched the pocket of his cargo shorts and scrounged out a roll of marijuana that was already wrapped. He set fire to it and dragged deeply. None of them would dare to come out tonight to find out who was smoking a joint behind the house. It was too dangerous. Night in this neigbourhood had teeth. The fangs of a cobra. He thought of the snake tattoo that he planned to get next week. The head of the creature would be on his left pectoral, its body would wrap round his front, and terminate in its tail at his back. A symbol of strength and cunning. He smiled again.

He jumped back in surprise as a large snake slithered suddenly from the dark, scrubby growth beside the perimeter wall. Dibi tensed and canvassed his immediate surroundings in his mind without moving a muscle. The cobra stood, swayed deliberately from side to side, its cold eyes fixed and staring, forked tongue flicking in and out. Yes. There was a wooden staff that his mother used for turning *tuwo*, leaning on the wall just within reaching distance to his left. He lunged for it, and the cobra struck with shocking speed in one seamless movement. He felt a sharp pain in the hand reaching for the turning stick, hit the ground screaming and jerked awake covered with sweat. He had fallen asleep on the stairs. He muttered beneath his breath. Curses born of fear.

Holding unto his right hand, he slid into the house, now completely dark. He heard sobbing - his mother - and oozed past her turned back into the passage leading to his room. As he closed the door noiselessly, he could hear her praying:

"Lord, please help me. My first born son, Lord. You promised I shall not cast my young."

Dibi slammed the pillow on his ear to cut out her babbling, now fainter through the shut door.

A hand jerked him from the bed, slammed him on his feet, flipped him effortlessly to face the stained wall of the room, and he saw something like a screen open on the wall. With a detached part of his mind, Dibiuno thought to himself that this was turning out to be quite a night. What was inside the "hot" he drank at Mama Anthony's eat-out this night for God's sake? His attention fully on the wall, he watched a child born on the screen. He watched the same child running to school with two friends. Mbidoka and Krubo. The child looked happy. He sang *Jesus loves me this I know* in a high, girlish voice. The voice seemed to come from an immense distance.

The scene faded to a young man running, stumbling, running, the wail of a police siren in the background. He turned a corner sharp right, saw a gun go off, felt a boring pain in his left temple, felt himself falling, falling falling... A white casket. He felt so much pity for the young man lying there. He walked over softly to the casket, looked in and saw in one blinding instant of recognition, his own face. No mortician's makeup could hide the hole in the left temple. He was still screaming as The End slid silently across the screen.

Dibi woke up screaming.

It was that same day that he met Makodi, a pretty neighbourhood girl he had been eyeing, at the corner shop. She was dressed in a straight skirt with polka dot blouse, and had a scarf tied round her hair. She looked good enough to eat, but she was hugging a Bible to her chest and walking rather fast. Two discouraging indices. Never one to give up without a fight, though, Dibi lounged over, head splitting from the disturbances of last night.

"Kai!"

She turned with an uncertain look on her face. Dibi was used to girls looking terrified when he hove in view. She didn't seem afraid, however, just questioning. He inched over, head throbbing like drum rhythms from an afrobeat song.

"Are you not Maki from the next street?" She seemed even more surprised that he knew her name.

"Yes?" She still had that neutral look on her face. Her eyes scanned his form. The tattoos, the mohawk. She shrugged. "I think I have seen you around too. You are Pastor Orasi's bad son *abi*?" She smiled disarmingly.

Dibi found himself smiling back sheepishly instead of slapping her across her insolent mouth. He looked around to make sure that no one had overheard their conversation.

"You look as if you are in a hurry? Are you going to church?" He was shocked at the hesitancy in his own voice. A mosaic of scenes from yesterday night suddenly scuttled through his mind and he blinked from the pain in his head.

She nodded and made as if to move on. He thought of grabbing her hand. Something stopped him. "Look," he stammered, "wait, let me just buy something for headache at this medicine store, I will go with you." Mentally, he turned and stared at himself in disbelief. Did he just offer to accompany this girl to church?

She nodded quickly, smiling, and didn't seem at all ashamed to be seen with him as they walked briskly to the nearby church. Passersby turned and looked at both of them curiously as they went by.

"In him was light and no darkness at all. He came to set the captives free. Ever since the serpent deceived Adam and Eve. Did not come to condemn the world, but that the world through him might be saved. The soul that sinneth shall die."

The sentences came to Dibi in a ragged rhythm that drilled into his skull. Then, Dibi watched himself hurrying. Rushing to the altar; saw faintly, the alarmed faces on both sides of the aisles staring at him. Found himself kneeling, sweating, crying, ripping with his nails at the tattoos on his arms...

Dibi broke the Code that evening. He fell into the light, walked back to his pew, sat down next to her, and heard Makodi sobbing and saying over and over, "Thank you Jesus! Thank you Jesus! He was there. Exactly where you showed me he would be!"

—— SHARED HUMANITY ——

This earth is green; all over it,
we walk and preen

Sauntering its corridors, strutting and
prancing like matadors

Our pride a red flag
That's about as valuable as slag

Never seeing in others' pain
Something that looks like our own chain

Look again, that stranger resembles you
Search his eyes, and you'll see
something of yourself too

─── **PEOPLE LIKE US** ───

Like a fingernail screeching across a blackboard, the sound came again. It finally scratched Lima into full consciousness and he realised what it was as he jerked his head to the left. In one quick movement, he slid his iPhone into his front pocket, pushed open the door and roared at the urchin, "get the … out of here!"

The boy who couldn't have been more than six bolted like an antelope on the Serengeti, and Lima dropped his gaze to the driver's door. Half his mind pre-occupied with breaking news about a fresh bomb blast in Maiduguri that he had been following on his device, it had taken a while for him to realize what had been making the irritating noise. Along with intoning: *"Abeg sir, abeg sir"* in a high pitched nasal voice, the little boy had been scratching at the door of his brand new Kia Optima with a bottle crown. The resulting design wasn't pretty.

Just as the advert executive was about to release another choice expletive, the street exploded into chaos. A yellow taxi cab shooting out of Marina Drive clipped the escaping young culprit, hesitated and roared off down Main Line. One Mazda car and a man in a Sienna gave chase but soon returned empty. These taxis knew the neighbourhood like Google Earth and the perpetrator had suddenly turned a sharp right down a busy street leaving his pursuers standing.

The small boy lay on the side of the street where he had fallen, looking like a ragged little bundle. Was he even alive? Several persons in the crowd bent to see. He was breathing, but nobody wanted police *wahalla*. Most certainly, there would be plenty of that for anyone who took the child to the hospital. The police would demand to know who the hit-and-run driver was. Suspiciously, they would glare at the Good Samaritan who brought the boy in and accuse him straight off of being the guilty party. If not, why had he taken the child to hospital?

Lima started to cross the road back to his abused car, but an image of babyish lashes on a grazed cheek stopped him dead in his tracks. Teeth gritted, he spun on his heel and re-crossed the street to where the crowd was still gawping at the child's body. No policeman in sight. A smear of blood daubed the kerb near the child's head. He scooped up the boy effortlessly, crossed the street for the third time that day, and gently deposited the small body on the rear seat of the car. He reflected that at least, one thing seemed to have turned out well today – not having cloth seats.

He verbally swatted off about three men who proposed to join him for the trip to the hospital, probably to make sure he wasn't taking off with the young victim to do some dastardly deed to or with him. He allowed a dark skinned middle aged woman in a *buba* top to climb into the front seat, though, just to pacify the suspicious crowd and they u-turned unto Herbert Macaulay

Way, hitting eighty almost immediately.

Near Cypress Specialist Hospital, the closest hospital to the accident site, the woman who had been sitting quietly suddenly turned to Lima. A quick glance right showed him tired features that had once been pretty. Her voice was low and almost masculine.

"You are a very kind man," she said. "I was there throughout. I fry *akara* and yam at that street corner. I saw everything that happened."

Lima grunted. He was not feeling very kind. If anything, he was feeling rather picked upon by fate.

She continued in her low, pleasant voice, "If I didn't know better, I would say you were an angel. Plus you are driving a white car." She laughed at her own joke.

It suddenly struck him that he was sitting in his car with a half-dead beggar boy and an *akara* seller, hardly his usual kind of companions, and that this was not all. This clearly "economically challenged" woman was speaking to him in almost flawless English. How?

Interest piqued, he suspended his deliberate silence, "Madam, you are educated?"

She nodded. She smiled at his hesitation. "How did I end up frying *akara* and yam by the road side?" She smiled again, mysteriously; "young man, everyone has a story. The boy in your backseat has one too, no doubt." She said nothing more after that.

Lima reflected that nothing in his twenty seven years of privileged la de dah upbringing to borrow his girlfriend, Sophie's, description of his family background got you ready for this.

He jumped an oozing gutter thick with biological growth. The smell coming off this fetid channel seemed to be a combination of decomposed ammonia and sulphur, yet, crooked legged tables loaded with produce bordered it on both sides. The plank meant for crossing over had long rotted into the slime. Loud music clashed in the dusty air from what passed as shops, and electric bulbs displayed a bilious yellow glow as if they were not sure they actually wanted to see the environment they were meant to light up.

No. 5 Rima Road was a mud hut ambitiously plastered with cement. The tin roof was a patchwork in the gloom. Tentatively, Lima lifted the shredded once-green curtain aside, stepped on the broken upper step to avoid the black slime in the gutter too close to the lower riser, and entered the single room. He looked around him helplessly, and wondered why on earth he was here.

The voice that had invited him to step in said "good evening" politely and nothing more. An uncomfortable silence ticked in. He looked at the woman. She was young, maybe in her late twenties, and badly dressed, but there was a quiet dignity about her. She stared at him with eyes full of inquiry. "Yes?" she said finally. "Are you Mr. Lima?" Lima nodded. "Please sit down." She shifted the baby in her arms slightly and pushed a stool toward him with her foot. Suddenly she smiled. "Please sorry if I seem rude. I only know that you nearly killed my son, Bekari. That is all I know about you."

Lima sat nonplussed. "I nearly killed your son? Madam, without me, your son would have died."

She shrugged.

For the second time in a few days, he suddenly startled. He watched her shift the tiny baby to nurse, and wondered,

"You speak well. Did you go to school?" For a heartbeat, she watched him with large, thoughtful eyes.

"I finished at Michaella Preparatory School in Wuson Heights."

"What? How, how…"

"How did my son end up begging on the streets? How did I end up a beggar myself?"

Thoughts swirling, Lima looked at her, impatient to hear.

"Dad was quite rich. He died in my final year. His only brother didn't want me and my mum around. We got on well on our own until mum died as well. Came across Ibe who said he loved me, and would get me a visa to Italy. Turned out he was a pimp. He's Bekari's father. Rape. I found my way back and decided I'd rather die than continue to be a prostitute. That's how we ended up on the streets."

She shrugged. Her expression matter of fact. "No, this baby is not Ibe's own. He's the Son of Poverty. By the way, thanks for nearly killing Bekari; your money since then has been very useful. Will you be his father? Looks like God has chosen you."

Lima nodded without meaning to. She smiled, turned away, and placed the Son of Poverty gently in a wooden box.

—— **CONFLICTED** ——

Here I stand in the field of fear
Staring adversity down
Looking terror in the eyeballs
And spitting at my dread

Here I stand on the edge of dawn
Wings folded and at rest
Waiting to unfurl, take a leap
And span the lightening sky

Here I stand in the reckoning
Pleading my cause, begging for justice

Voice raised in pitiful supplication
To deaf ears in a head turned aside,

Here I stand struggling to find
the part of me that's "right"
that answers the need of the hour...
Have I somehow lost myself?

Am I Fighter?
Angel?
Or this pitiful Victim?

—— THE PERFECT BODY ——

"And one and one and two and two…" The chant rose and fell from the trainer in the front of the gym. "And kick and kick, step back, yes, one one…" Binu felt her heart pounding like a pestle punishing yam for an afternoon meal. Was she getting a cardiac? It certainly felt as if her heart was about to go on strike permanently.

She viewed the trainer with misplaced dislike. *She* looked as if she ate leaves and rusks morning, noon and night – and what is more, enjoyed doing it. With one more triumphant yell, the woman performed an effortless split, flicked off the music and told the gym class, "That's it for today. Wednesday same time." Binu hissed inside. The trainer wasn't even breathing hard!

The twenty eight year old grasped her knees and leaned down to draw in life-giving oxygen in gulps. She was not fit and she was not fine. She looked in the bathroom mirror on her way through the gym's conveniences as she headed for her gym bag stashed in a corner and a tired ride home. The reflection she saw there made her draw in her lower lip with disapproval.

Her overweight cheeks looked back at her without remorse. The features were alright, you might say. Humorous eyes set a bit wide apart, a cute nose, well cut lips with a bonus cleft in a determined chin. Yes people had even called her beautiful, but for the life of her, all she could see was this extra wadding everywhere. She hissed and picked up her towel.

Day one of her weight loss journey had just ended. Binu was tired but triumphant.

All through secondary school, she had been that tall, skinny senior that everybody called *kpelenge* including junior students when she was just out of ear shot. What happened? She wasn't quite sure, but throughout university, the finger on the bathroom scales kept pointing onward and downward until she realized she wasn't just comfortably padded anymore, she was F-A-T. Like her mother's people. Big hips, big bottom, the works. Binu hissed again.

She turned the key in the lock of her self-contained unit housing, stepped into a space that for her had always represented the definition of success. Nice neighbourhood, potted plants, sweet peach and green décor, her own private nest. She looked at the cabbage and carrots waiting on the kitchen counter to be shredded and eaten for dinner and sighed. No more late-night sandwiches and soda, no more tuwo with hot okro soup at 9 pm after working late in the office. Oh well. *Wetin man for do?* If life threw you a challenge, you faced it.

Talking about challenges, she remembered her conversation with Aunty Meji last week:

"*Binu wetin dey happen now?*" Her aunt had begun.

"Ma, I don't understand. What is happening to…?"

"To you my dear." Aunty smiled sarcastically. "Your *oyibo ma* is too much. How come you finished law school four years ago, have a good job, and you're yet to call us to tie *gele*? When are you getting married *abeg*?"

"Ah aunty, will I marry myself? I am waiting for God o!"

"Continue waiting until you are over thirty. And please while you're waiting, lose weight. No one wants to marry a bag of cassava these days."

Bag of cassava! The memory of that conversation filled Binu with heat. She almost hated the nagging, interfering woman. Imagine! What kind of talk was this? Did she create herself? Why had God even decided to suddenly make her fat? She thought of blaming God, then decided against it. Just go and find a gym and finally do something about it, lose this weight. Thus the sortie to the gym.

Then again, there was this marriage matter. That, in itself, was beginning to rankle. It was starting to burn like acid on bare skin. How many of your friends' bridal and baby showers do you have to attend before you start feeling old?

Binu watched Sarah, from the accounts department, eat through a huge plate of vegetable soup and pounded yam laced with assorted meats. Why do some people get away with it, and some don't? Sarah was as thin as a blood-starved mosquito but she could put it away like a labourer. Where was the justice?

As she was picking desultorily over a coleslaw minus mayonnaise, Binu felt eyes on the back of her head, almost a physical touch. Nonchalantly, she glanced in the mirror and yes, it was him, the new man in admin. Young, single – she had checked – and very eligible. So what next? Mentally, her lips turned down. Not thin enough. No contest. Thin girls win! Fat girls to the mat. Contest over. She swung her bag over her shoulder and marched to the canteen door.   At least, Binu thought bitterly, there was still the job. That kept her focused and motivated. For now, she was married to the job for better for worse.   Marriage to a man could wait, she had a career to build and an urgent brief to prepare.

"Let me help you with that." A warm, male voice spoke surprisingly close to her, and she jumped. Binu hadn't noticed him approach because she was wrestling with three shopping bags and the car's remote control. It was Eric, Mister Young, Single and Eligible from the office, and Binu gladly surrendered two of the bags in order to get the car door open.

Great friendships start with just one hello. So this was how it felt to meet that other person who touched all the right spots, heart, mind and soul? Who beat the sparks from the anvil? Binu found herself smirking. Quick work! Barely how many months of gyming up and the results were right here already. She reflected that in her chubby days, Eric would never have given her another glance, probably gone for the wispy Sarah or one of those other NEPA poles in the office.

One glorious day several months later, she decided to make sure...

With a view of the darkening beach, a lover's moon just beginning to do its thing in the heavens and a cool breath of air taming the day's heat as backdrop, she asked coquettishly,

"What drew your gaze? My toned – ok - toning arms, or was it my new size twelve silhouette?"

Eric smiled. "Yes. I would say it has to have been your perfect body…"

This wasn't quite what Binu had hoped for. Could it be, after all, that the perfect man was, God forbid it, shallow? She eyed him uncertainly.

"Binu I fell in love with you over a year ago when you were, what? A size eighteen?" He smiled as Binu gave him a punch in the arm.

"We met for the first time at a church service, or make that I saw you for the first time at Simi's wedding thanksgiving in Christ the Redeemer's church; not here in the office."

Binu's mouth would have hung open if she wasn't too much of a lady. She was a size twenty then!

"I knew then that you were my wife. I saw a woman beautiful in and out. When you sang 'How Great thou Art' as soloist, I fell in love with a woman with the perfect body – the perfect spiritual body... You are beyond body beautiful sweetheart. I wasn't surprised to walk into Access

Properties and find you there. I just knew we would meet again. "

That's when Binu's mouth did swing open. She just stopped herself from scratching her weave in addition. What? All the crazy days in the gym for nothing? He fell in love with her when she was FAT?

Oh well, she reflected, at least her heart hadn't hammered like it used to when they'd climbed the stairs to this lookout point over the beach.

It was hammering now, again, though. Violently. Somehow Eric was on one knee with a ring in his hand saying words she couldn't hear...

A Woman's Burden

—— SLAPS AND PATS ——

Will you spend your time

eating the lime of hate?

When you found your mate

And you thought he was fine

Did you know, could you know,

That a blow is nothing to him?

Slaps and pats

Pats and slaps

this and then that; next a tine

thrust in the pate

Nothing at all to him?

Now, tears flow red

Though bride price is paid

Sister, will you stay or plan to flay?

— JUST THE TWO OF YOU —

"You don't have more sense than an ant do you?" Obimra stared at Chinwendu with a casual insolence that infuriated her to the very marrow of her bones, but she knew better than to say anything.

The last time she replied to his pointed verbal barbs, he had beaten her so thoroughly that she looked like she had been in an *okada* accident. That was one week ago. Since then, she had bid her time. She watched him like a hawk watches a small yellow chick. Watched his chest rise and fall as he breathed, looked at his nostrils flare as he got angry just watching her watching him. She looked at the curve of his back as he slept turned away from her in the light of the street lamps and she loved him, but she hated him too and she waited.

Her mind drifted to their wedding. It had been everything a romantic girl like her could have wished. Soft peach and ivory hues cascaded in shimmering folds from the ceiling and reflected in the lace blouses and *geles* of her guests and in her three-tiered wedding cake. The buffet table strained under the weight of the food, and again, she saw herself in her mental portraits of that day, waving, hugging, smiling misty eyed at all these people gathered to honour Obimra and her. That joy should have lasted a lifetime...

She could not remember why he had hit her the first time. All she could feel then was not even the force of the blow that landed her on her behind and brought tears to her eyes, but the indescribable pain as something delicate and precious recoiled inside her and died. She stared at him horrified; waited for him to say something, to apologise, to say "Nma, I didn't mean it, I don't know what happened". He simply glared at her, snatched his car keys off the top of the fridge and then she heard his Mercedes start up and reverse angrily on the gravel, spitting chips as he left.

On her wedding day, the pastor, a stocky dark man with a sharp haircut had turned to her with a dramatic gesture. "Chinwendu, look beside you; how many people do you see?" Smiling, looking deep into Obim's eyes, she had replied, "just one." Pastor grinned with satisfaction. "Keep it that way. Don't let a third party into your matter. No matter what happens, solve it between the two of you. Pray and find the solution between just the two of you. No third parties."

She had gone to that same pastor with a bruised eye, eight months after the wedding. He looked shocked. She saw overwhelming pity in his eyes, but also a wariness as if he really didn't want to get involved. After she had broken down, sobbing, with Pastor patting her shoulder comfortingly, the message was still the same. "Go home. Remember, just the two of you."

Chinwendu had tried to pray, but the gall, the pain, robbed her of expression in the place of prayer. Increasingly, dark, suffocating thoughts overwhelmed her. She woke from frequent nightmares, shaking and covered with sweat. She felt trapped, strangled, violent.

Tears streaming silently from her eyes, Chinwe touched a wary hand to a bald spot at the top of her braided hair. The pain was more in her heart than in her scalp. She looked again at the packet in her hand. It had the picture of a dried rat on it; black on red. With a quick gesture, she shook all the contents into the pot and stirred it with a hand that no longer shook.

She walked over to the door of the bedroom, knocked quietly, called out, "Obim, dinner is on the table," dished two plates and sat down to wait.

WIDOW

Hair is matted with old dirt
As I sit on the bare floor nursing my
pain
Gathering and tucking in a faded skirt,
Legs shake unconsciously with inner
strain

My eyes stare, but I grasp nothing
All I see is the deep darkness within my
head
I hear noises all around, as they mutter
something

"We must see to it that she leaves this homestead"

"She is a witch, she knows what happened."
I struggle in vain to shake my head
How can I kill this man on whom my life depends?
Do all women become witches when their husbands are dead?

My heart is screaming
My eyes are throbbing
My head is pounding
My body is trembling

If only they will leave me alone
Perhaps I can die quietly too, anon

———— ACCUSED ————

My Loneliness is much worse in a crowd. How can you reach out when your heart is dry and dying? Who

do you reach out to, when you are

surrounded by people displaying

hatred, prominent as a tumour that is flourishing on the forehead?

Amara looked over at the corner near the banana grove standing close to the grave. The trees stretched their broad green arms over the disturbed red earth as if to protect it. The bunches of green bananas hanging from the trees seemed contradictory. How could so much life exist in the presence of death?

She slid her gaze to her feet, and noted absently that her chocolate nail polish was chipped. She wiggled her toes inside the simple white slippers she was wearing, as if to convince herself she was not paralyzed. That she was still capable of movement, and that this was not a bad dream that her phone alarm would soon dismiss, waking her to a brand new and most importantly, normal morning.

Her thoughts were interrupted by

a friend from Abuja, Ifedi Ojukwu, greeting her from across the widow's barrier. She dredged up a watery smile, surprised to see her. Grateful she had been able to come. Demarcated from sympathizers by a low wooden fence, Amara sat surrounded by kinswomen she barely knew. She could feel waves of animosity coming from most of them. These were women with whom she attended her village women's meetings whenever she was at home. One or two of them, she considered friends.

Her brother-in-law had been

business like. "Amara, we want you to tell us what happened to our brother. That is all. I know that two weeks

before, you talked him into writing a will and two weeks later, he had an encounter with assassins and died. For the rest, it is only you that know."

Amara held her aching heart in her hands. Struggled for composure. Tried to find the right words; failed, and burst into tortured wails that rang off the walls of her living room. Her brother-in-law, her husband's younger brother, whom they had paid fees for through university, and who had always called her aunty, stared at her coldly and dispassionately as if she was a strange object he was trying to configure.

That was her introduction to widowhood. Sleepless nights gave way to busy days of planning the burial. Several times a day, she wondered whose burial she was planning. How could this be? She had always told him she would go first because she would not be able to survive without him and he would label her selfish, and laughingly say no, he would go first; and now he had. Suddenly. Just like that.

She watched sympathizers moving into the compound group by group; some with colourful wrappers to add to a growing pile on her brother-in-law's left hand. One or two carried jute ropes to show they had brought the price of a cow as condolence.

Some women came to cut her hair as was customary, and she refused. They glared at her like wounded lions robbed of their prey. She held firm. Who knew what they would do with the cut hair? Stories abounded of widows who did not survive their husband's burial by more than a year. Sickening and dying from nobody was sure exactly what. People would murmur that it was deep sorrow. *Mgbawa obi*. Amara thought to herself that she could not afford to die of a "broken heart" with two teenage girls depending on her now that Ikem was gone.

She thought of Okeamaka and Ifeoma, her two daughters, briefly back from the United States for the burial; and imagined them desolate in her mother's home across town. She had left them there to protect them. Too much was at stake. Far too much; not least, the fact that there was no male heir. These two girls were all that stood between "them" and the money, and though the girls hardly counted, not being male, yet they were his children, and all the relevance she still had in the Okoye family.

She and Ikem had married a few years out of university. She was twenty four, and he was six years older. Amara thought of all she had gone through in those early years. She had any number of suitors to choose from, her mother fondly called her *ugegbe nwanyi* because of her light skinned beauty, but for Amara, it was always going to be Ikem and no one else. They had built what they had from scratch. In addition to her law practice, she opened a dressmaking shop which did very well, while Ikem went from one job to the other, using her finances as a cushion, restlessly seeking the exact fit he wanted.

Then it came, a prime job with a multinational company. They moved to an upscale part of Abuja into a large house which became a Mecca for relatives. In her mind, Amara called her new home Open House Hotel.

Sometimes, they had as many as five people staying with them. These distant relatives would go home and gossip about the fact that Amara and her husband had a swimming pool and a cook. As if they had not sweated for every single thing they had.

A woman staggered in, wailing that death was wicked. Stocky and dark, she tried to rush over and throw herself on the grave, but was restrained by concerned bystanders. She composed a dirge on the spot and sang it feelingly and mournfully. However, a few minutes later, Amara saw her out of the corner of her eye, and the same dark, short and ample woman was laughing with Mama Bennet and complaining that an usher had given her only *ukwa* without the bitterleaf soup she wanted to taste as well. The usher tried to explain that the bitterleaf soup had finished, and finally pacified the angry mourner with a bottle of cold malt drink.

Inwardly, Amara hissed. Outside, she looked up. Clouds were gathering and although it was getting to evening now, the humid heat was stifling. It would rain. The heavens would mix their tears with hers today, and it would be entirely appropriate. Shame on those who said they had gone to

see rainmakers. She was glad their gods were about to disgrace them comprehensively. Their boast had been that it would not rain throughout the burial ceremonies.

She faced him across the living room. "I will go back to Abuja on Saturday."

"What did you say?" Ikenna, her husband's brother, looked at her like a germ under a microscope.

"I said I will go back to Abuja on Saturday, there is nothing left for me to do here."

"Who will receive those who are coming to console you over your husband's death?"

Amara shrugged, "you and your sisters will receive them. I have to return to work so that I can take care of my children."

"The moment you walk through that door without my permission on Saturday, consider yourself no longer a member of this family."

"Ikenna, you and your sisters cancelled me from your family the moment your brother died, so that is really not a threat." Amara adjusted her white mourning wrapper and wished him goodnight.

The new widow looked at the screen of her laptop again. She reached a shaky hand for the cup of coffee sitting near it and drank a quick mouthful. She was drinking too much coffee these days. Her nerves vibrated like the shoulders of a maiden dancing *nkwa umu agbogho*. Blinding headaches came and left.

She was re-reading an email from Ikenna who had not called her since she left the village to ask if she had arrived safely. She, Ikem's wife, was to organize the papers for all their landed property in Lagos and Port Harcourt, and give him a feedback by email in the next three weeks so that he could decide what to do with them as executor of Ikem's estate.

Amara bit her lip. Rubbed her aching eyes, and turned with irritation to her phone that was buzzing on vibration mode. She picked it up absently without checking who was on the line.

"Hello, Amaechi here." The voice sounded teasing, and Amara felt her pent up rage reach gagging level.

"What do you want?" She asked without grace. The man she had always thought was one of her husband's closest friends, whose wife she sometimes went out shopping with, continued,

"Don't sound like that. I know you're lonely, and I just want to talk."

"What do you want to talk about?" Hardly holding herself back from hissing like an infuriated cobra.

"The fact that I like you. Always have."

Amara killed the call, put the phone on airplane mode and threw it on the nearby sofa. She turned back to the

laptop, resting her aching head on the heel of her left hand and took   another sip of her cooling coffee. It was not just Amaechi. There were several other men buzzing around her like bees around a hive. She could never have imagined that several of the people she and Ikem called friends wanted

nothing more than to get into bed with her, their friend's wife. Or was it just widowhood that had made her twice as attractive? She felt a warm tear roll down her face and wiped it with the back of her hand.

One colleague in the office had even offered her a trip to Dubai if she would rendezvous with him at Hotel Excelsior. A trip to Dubai! Amara nearly smiled through her tears. She went to Dubai every three months or so to stock the fabric unit of her dressmaking outfit. She thought ruefully to herself, have I become so cheap, a mere prostitute? So this was part of the price of widowhood?

Her mind went back yet again to a strange call she had received yesterday.

The number was hidden. Whoever it was had also disguised their voice.

According to the caller, Ikenna knew something about Ikem's death. The caller was struggling to live with their conscience. Ikem was a good man. He didn't deserve to go this way. Before Amara could gather her shocked wits about her, whoever it was had cut off the call.

Trucaller revealed nothing. She stared around her, unseeing, at the ash and charcoal grey decor of her living room, her thoughts turning in circles like a carousel.

She had wondered what sort of bad luck it was for Ikem to make his will and be killed two weeks later, making her a prime suspect in police investigations. What if the voice on the phone was speaking the truth? What if Ikenna really knew something about his brother's death? After all, Ikem had made him the executor of the will, and that was how he knew about a will being written.

Amara thought deeply. If Ikenna was a murderer, then she and her daughters were in more danger than she knew. At almost one billion, she and Ikem's combined assets were enough to kill for if you had no conscience. But Ikenna had never

given off the vibes of a conscienceless murderer. Could this be true? Just then, it was as if she heard her grandmother's voice in her head: "*Ana ede ya n'iru?*" Do they write it on the face? Whenever as children they expressed shock that someone they knew could have done this or that terrible thing, Nne always asked that question: Do they write what someone is capable of doing on their forehead?

Amara decided that same instant what she would do. She walked over to the file cabinet where all the property papers were kept. Ikem had always been meticulous. Dragged out folders. Walked quickly over to the kitchen closet, pulled down an empty beverage carton, dumped the files into the carton, walked back to her laptop, tapped on an airline flight booking app and began to type rapidly.

—— **DIVORCE** ——

The heat haze made the images dance in the distance. It baked out the last drops of dew from her body. The painful sequence continued: One heavy foot in front of the other. Rest. One more labored step. Gasping for oxygen, labouring to breathe, leaning forward in her quest, the city coming nearer then moving further away, approaching and diminishing into the distance.

"I will never get there." Realization dawned, and with it a desperate sadness that broke out from her throat first as a croak, then as a wail. Nnenna woke up, rasping out a cry that felt like grated copra as it left her insides. Harsh and dry. She realized she was still gasping for air, and began to draw in long calming breaths. Slowly. Inhale, exhale... Gradually, her heartbeat was slowing to normal.

The dreams were becoming more frequent, and Nnenna did not need an interpreter to tell her what they meant. Her dreams spoke of loss, of the unattainable. Happiness was bleeding away from her like blood oozing from a deep cut. She was dying.

She looked at the display screen of her phone. The time was 2 am in the middle of the night. She knew she would not sleep again. Coughing to clear her dry throat, she reached for her *Bible*, opened to Psalm 30 and began to read: *"Hear, O Lord, and have mercy upon me: Lord, be thou my helper."*

The tears came, then. Heavy drops of pain that fell unto the open page. Each drop puckered the place where it landed, drawing it into ridges like her heart. She made no attempt to stop them falling like April rain.

A gentle tap on her door. She quickly

pulled up the neck of her nightdress and used it to wipe her face. Michelle came in, shutting the door quietly behind her.

"Mummy?" It was a question and a plea at the same time. Nnenna moved in so that her fifteen year old could sit on the edge of the bed. She managed a watery smile to reassure her baby who was already growing into a beautiful young woman. Michelle leaned in and put her arms around her. Rocked her, as if Nnenna was the infant, and she the mother.

"Mummy, you can't go on crying. Let daddy go. We don't want him to be part of our lives. We don't need him.

"Shhhh! Don't say that." Nnenna gently disengaged herself, swung her legs over the edge of her bed and walked into the bathroom. Quickly, she used the toilet then turned to stare at her face in the bathroom mirror. She was aging prematurely and her daughter was growing up too quickly. Seeing too much. She sighed. A deep, bitter sigh from the pit of her stomach.

She bent to splash some cold water from the sink on her face. Cleaned it briskly with a towel, and stepped out. Michelle was lying down on the other side of the bed. She would not leave this night. Nnenna knew it would be no use asking her to. She sighed, got into bed, felt Michelle put her head on her shoulder, as she lay there staring at the ceiling, willing sleep to come.

Death comes bit by bit. A branch that is cut off and thrown out doesn't die immediately. It crumbles back to the dust slowly. That pretty much described all she had left with Mike, something green on the outside and dead on the inside.

He had left again yesterday after a bitter quarrel. Walked out. He must have gone either to a hotel or to Rose, his latest girlfriend. She lived in a smart, upscale two-bedroom apartment in a posh area of town. He was paying. He had also bought her a

Mercedes. Nnenna had all the evidence carefully stored away in photographs she had taken of the damning images on his phone using her own phone camera. He had no idea she knew his password.

She had flinched as she came across a folder on his phone with nude photographs of Rose. Disgusted and almost nauseated, she clicked away with her phone camera, storing evidence for she was not sure exactly what.

"Are you ok?" She came back from a long distance to see her boss, Mr. Okafor, looking at her with concern. How long had he been standing there, trying to hand her that paper?

"I didn't sleep very well. I'm sorry. No NEPA. I only slept off this morning." She realized she was babbling. "Sorry let me have them. Are they the estimates?" He handed over the document with another long and inscrutable stare and walked out her cubicle, leaving the door open. She got up to shut it. Sat down. Tried to engage with the figures on the page, drifted in and out of her thoughts. Her eyes rested on the framed photograph of Mike, Michelle and Michael. It had been taken during a holiday in Britain. She looked at Mike. Handsome fellow. That had always been part of the problem with this marriage. She picked up the photograph and placed it face down on the table. Reached for her handbag on the floor beside her desk. Might as well go for lunch, it was almost break time.

Never a particularly chatty person, Nnenna found herself these days wanting more and more to be alone with her thoughts. She ordered jollof rice, plantain and chicken and edged to a corner table where she could sit alone and eat in peace.

"Na wa o! So you wan occupy one table only you?" Nnenna tried to keep the frustration out of her face. She smiled a weak smile and waved her hand to

signal Nkem to go ahead and sit down if she wanted. She wondered why some people were born with all the sensitivity of an elephant's hide.

Nkem sat down, smiling irrepressibly. *"You are looking one kin one kin.* Did you sleep at all last night?" She went on to suggest cucumber and all sorts of treatments for dark circles. She didn't seem to care that Nnenna was contributing nothing so far to the conversation.

"Like me now, nothing disturbs my sleep o!" She continued, "even the first days after my divorce, I still slept like the sleeping beauty I am." She cackled at her own joke and swallowed a lump of garri nicely covered with Egusi soup.

"This is the first time I am hearing that you are divorced."

Having said that, Nnenna ruefully asked herself, 'how would you know? You avoid the woman.' So all this bright cheerfulness hid a tragedy of this proportion? An amputation.

"Five years this March." Nkem ate a piece of smoked fish. "My sister, the psychiatric hospital is directly behind my house. Three quarters of the patients there are women, and almost all of them, it is their husbands and their marriages that sent them there. My friend works there as a nursing sister, so I should know. Nne, I didn't want to join them, so I left that bastard called Chukelu. I am taking care of my children and they lack nothing." She chewed noisily on a piece of cartilage, clearly enjoying her food and the conversation.

Nnenna speared a pea in her rice and munched it thoughtfully.

"I thought you are a deacon at Fountain of Life Assembly?"

Nkem raised a brow, "And so?"

"God says, 'I hate divorce.'"

The other woman laughed. "Where did you see it written in the Bible that God says 'I love suicide?' Chapter and verse o!"

For the rest of their lunch time,

Nkem rattled on and Nnenna listened. When one of their co-workers came over, she used the opportunity to escape back to the office. So Nkem was divorced? And there was no evidence of depression or high blood pressure? She wondered what was wrong with her, Nnenna. Was divorce really this freeing?

She reached over, cracked out two pills, threw them into her mouth and gulped down some water. Since Mike left again, her blood pressure had spiked. She could feel it. The blinding headaches that felt as if a blacksmith was hammering metal inside her head, the sleeplessness, the dizzy spells. She reached over and called her mother. *"Nne m kedu? Unu anokwa ofuma?"*

Her mother's cheerful voice always lifted her spirits. Seventy eight years old, but healthy and clear headed like someone twenty years younger, Nne Ora as they fondly called her, was a lifeline to all her four surviving children. She had buried two in her lifetime. Intensely spiritual, her prayer and fasting life were legendary. Nnenna had found herself wishing several times in her life that she had her mother's strength and resilience. She had never told her mother about Mike, but she suspected she knew.

"You are still awake?" She could

hear the concern in her mother's voice and tried to laugh lightly.

"I am getting to be like you, Mama. *Agadi nwanyi ula gwulu n'anya*," they had a good laugh over Mama's usual description of herself as an old woman with no sleep left in her eyes.

"That is me, but you are too young to be awake by this time. Where is Mike?"

Nnenna asked God to forgive her before she told the lie, "He travelled over some business in his office."

"*Eziokwu?*" Nne Ora did not sound convinced. "I had a dream yesterday night. You were trying to find your way to Umuchu. As you were struggling to cross that road to Nkwo Umuagu, it was as if a hand was holding you back. I could see a car coming toward you and I kept shouting '*nwa m, gbaba oso.*' I woke up shouting. It is not a good dream. I have been praying for you. Please fast and pray and tell Mike to join you."

Nnenna felt goose pimples stand on her arms. The same dream, over there in Onitsha. God had shown her mother her struggles. Should she tell her? She had never told her mother about the hell her marriage had become. She decided against it. It would feel like a betrayal. "Nne Ora, I will pray. Please be praying for me."

Nnenna decided to see her Pastor in his office. She was shown in and sat nervously in the consulting seat in the quiet, cream painted room. She knew Pastor Felix was surprised to see her. She had never been in his office for counselling since he was sent to lead this chapter of the church three years ago.

To her own shock, she suddenly blurted out, "What do you feel about divorce for a Christian?" That wasn't what she had meant to say at all. It seemed to jump out of her throat of its own will.

"Are you having problems in your marriage?" He looked at her without surprise like someone who had heard it all over years of ministry. She nodded and everything spilled out of her like a dam bursting its retaining walls. He sat and listened quietly.

"Is your husband not the leader of the Missions Finance Committee?"

Deeply embarrassed, Nnenna stared at the table, said yes, wished she hadn't come, that she was anywhere else but here. The clock on the wall ticked on slowly, counting off seconds of a life gone tragically wrong. Pastor Felix steepled his hands, seemed lost in thought, then he told her, "Please ask him to see me."

Nnenna reached for her phone three times before she dialled his number. "Yes?" The voice was cold. The voice of a total stranger. Her husband of twenty years. Mike.

"Good evening." Silence. "Mike I just have to say it, I am sorry I shouted at you the other day. I am very sorry." Silence; then, "Why are you calling?" His voice sounded like the sharp edge of a knife.

"Pastor Felix said he wants to see you over something to do with the Missions Finance Committee." Nnenna was shocked at how good she was becoming at lying. The seconds tapped on.

"Why didn't he call me directly?"

"I don't know."

Mike disconnected the call. In the silence that followed, Nnenna went downstairs to prepare a dinner of rice and stew for Michelle and herself. These days, with Michael away at university, the cooking was not challenging any more. Michelle wasn't much of an eater.

Michelle joined her in the kitchen, doing whatever she was told, watching her mother's face.

"Mummy where is daddy?"

Nnenna didn't turn from the rice she was washing. "I don't know."

"Why is he like this?" She could tell

Michelle was genuinely puzzled.

"Just pray for your daddy. He will be alright." She didn't know what else to say. They ate a mostly silent dinner.

Nnenna couldn't decide which part of this whole thing was most painful. Was it the damage to her self-esteem? The constant fear of failure, of people finding out what was going on in her home. The dreams, the illnesses - she seemed to have no immunity these days - or the confusion in her daughter's eyes as she tried to process what a fifteen year old had no call to be dealing with. One day, Michelle had told Nnenna, "When I grow up, I don't want to get married." Nnenna still remembered the sharp pain of that statement.

It was the evening of the next day, and Mike walked in through the front door. She could see the palm trees outside, their green fronds streaming behind them like the tresses of giant women fleeing from the wind. He slammed the door. She was in the living room, watching Jeopardy with Michelle, but the moment she looked in his face she sent a silent signal to her daughter to go to her room. The child left without greeting him.

"What did you go and tell Felix?" He demanded angrily.

"I told him what he should know as our pastor."

"Alright. Go and also tell him this: I have finished with this marriage. I want a divorce."

"I will never divorce you. Is it so that you can marry your Rose?"

She watched the shock ripple across his face. Suddenly she knew why she had subconsciously felt the need to gather the evidence. "Wait here." She walked upstairs, taking her time. Got her phone, came down, patted the settee beside her. He sat obediently.

She scrolled for a few minutes before he tried to snatch the device from her hand. Nnenna smiled sadly. "It doesn't matter what you do with the phone. Do you really think I am so stupid that it is only on this phone?"

Mike stared at her with grudging respect.

She asked him, "Do you still want a divorce? I don't believe in it, and neither do you, after all, you are the Chairman of the Missions Finance Committee and a good Christian." He stared at her, speechless.

"And if anything bad ever happens to me, just know that Pastor Felix has all the copies of everything on this phone."

She turned on her heel and went

upstairs. No, there would be no divorce.

—— The Mathematics ——
of Time

It is true that time surprises

I have even seen it subtract

and at other times add;

I have known time to pad

the sum

of the outcomes

It has sometimes divided choices

and opened up messes

hidden in human decisions

Indeed, it is true that time can heal,

but

did you know that time can also kill?

A Woman's Burden

———— REUNION ————

Weaving to the beat of the music, feeling him rub up against her, Hope danced as if this was the end. In her manicured right hand, she clutched a glass of martini, like a person drowning at sea holds unto a buoy. Occasionally, the alcohol splashed over the rim of the glass, making wet spots on the maroon, Italian tiles. They looked like patches of newly shed blood. She danced in and out of reality.

"You know, if you had asked me

all those years ago whose name we would be hearing everywhere,   I'd have said Hope's. And I was right."

They had cadged a table for six at The Cabana for their meet up after thirty years of leaving school. Six women hovering anywhere between forty five and fifty. Ifeoma looked around her as she spoke.

The Cabana, as usual, was full. Lights reflected off the metallic decor, and well trained waiters hovered over guests like concerned mother hens. She raised one exquisitely manicured forefinger and a steward dashed over immediately. Ify, as her friends called her, ordered two more plates of hors d'ouvre and reflected that marrying money had its distinct advantages. It could get you a table at the poshest restaurant in town even on a busy evening.

She looked around their table for six. The years had been kind to some, but not so kind to others like Mildred Isichei. Mildred had a harassed look hanging like an April cloud around her. She was dressed in the style of someone who had the right stuff but didn't have the state of mind needed to put them together. With several years' experience as a pediatric doctor, she was a financial success, but her home life? Ify shook her head mentally.

Mildred's home life was nothing to be jealous of. Her husband had this reputation for bedding anything wearing a bra, and there had been talk of a divorce.

Mildred could read Ify's thoughts off her face like an airport official reading a scan. She wondered why Ify had brought them together. Was it to mock people like her who had succeeded at failing or was it failed at succeeding? She was used to friends' pity and scorn by now. Her situation was no secret. Mildred's eyes moved to Ibime sitting next to Ify. She thought to herself that the years truly held change in their hands. She had last seen Ibime five years ago at the airport.

Mildred had been surprised to spot her former Zimbabwe dormitory bunk mate looking like she'd won the lottery. The handbag on her wrist alone, cost one point something. Mildred knew the real thing when she saw it. Ibime's complexion glowed like something used to pampering, and her casual outfit was flawless. She lifted an arm banded by chunky gold jewelry, patted a small natural Afro, then turned to speak to a handsome, dark, rather short man beside her. Mildred was fairly sure this was her husband. They looked like the original power couple, oozing confidence from every pore. Enough to give someone an inferiority complex if that someone was not careful.

She walked over with a fairly confident smile on her face. "Ibime?" This new and glossy version of her former classmate turned at the sound of her name. "Yes?" Mildred watched her face as she scanned through files in her mind. Office? No. Family? Obviously not. Church? Just as Mildred was about to help jog her memory, she said hesitantly, "Mildred? Mildred Isichei? Class 5B?" Then they were screaming and creating a scene in the terminal. Ibime's husband watched them, amused, waiting for both of them to calm down.

Before Ibime caught her flight to Lagos, they exchanged phone numbers and promised to see each other sometime, since they both lived in Abuja. There had been no meeting, not even a conversation since that day. Mildred looked over at Ibime. She was deep in conversation with Bisi on her left.

Her mind wandered back to Federal Government Secondary school. They had both arrived in school the next day after re-opening. Most of their brand new classmates who had come in the previous day looked and acted as if they had been in school for a week. They already spoke the school jargon fluently. Matron assigned both of them to the same double bunk. The only empty one left in the dormitory. They had both ended up in the B class as well.

She came to know the other girl fairly well. Her nickname, Area Scatter, said it all. Ibime was untidy. Uniform, school shoes, hair, class notes, just about everything. Her grades were never very far from failing either. Mildred remembered that Ibime's father was a junior civil servant, a clerk or something, in those days, and her mother a primary school teacher. Who could have looked into the future and seen this shiny person seated at the end of the table? She smiled involuntarily, and just then, Ibime caught her eye, smiled back, gave a half wave, and turned back to Bisi.

Mildred thought, "Who'd have imagined it? Poor kid makes it into the big league." She pulled herself up with a mental reprimand, "Mildred that is so unworthy of you. Are you jealous?" She sighed inwardly. Yes. She was jealous of all these women she barely knew any more. They were all happy except her. Money couldn't buy joy. Or peace, or love, or anything that truly mattered. The only thing that stopped her from leaving Paul was their three teenage children.

Toyin swirled her drink in her glass, and took another sip. Her favourite. A smooth, icy mixture of vodka and lime. She hadn't been going to have any tonight, but why not? It wasn't every opportunity she got to relax like this. Not like she was an alcoholic or anything. You genuinely had to have some help to skip through the minefield that was her workplace without being blown apart mentally on a daily basis. She took another sip. Looked at the other women talking, and let her mind drift. What would these women say if they knew how close she was to being taken into custody for a major financial crime? She wondered if any of them had the clout to help. Ibime looked like she might know everyone in government. The girls would all be so disappointed. They had received a strict moral upbringing in school. Not necessarily Christian, but principled and straight. She took another absent minded sip of her drink and looked at the other ladies. Everyone seemed to have done very well for themselves. She listened to the laughter around the table as Ifeoma shared a tale out of school as she called it, listened to the clink of eager cutlery and tried to smile. She could almost feel the noose around her neck. Toyin didn't have much of an appetite tonight. She wished she could call it a night. She was getting a headache, but leaving would look anti-social and ungrateful. She wondered how much Ifeoma was paying for their meal. Not that she looked as if money could ever be an issue. Toyin had spied her Cabana gold card when she opened her purse to pull out her iPhone.

Bisi glanced sideways at Toyin. They had never gotten along even in school, and had had one or two cat fights on their alumni social media platform recently. Always been something about that girl. Bisi mentally shrugged her shoulders. That you went to school with someone didn't mean you had to be their friend.

She wondered how true it was that the anti-graft agency was trailing their classmate. Someone in Toyin's office had told her there would be a major media blowout soon. Bisi reflected that such a thing would be bad for the image of the school. Maybe, just maybe, for the sake of the alma mater, she should try to help this woman out. She had the connections, tentacles winding through government offices and agencies. She put down her drink and excused herself to use the conveniences.

"Such a nice girl, that Bisi. She knows every big man in this town one on one. She is a correct big girl. She can fix anything."

Mildred looked at Ifeoma with distaste. Was this what this evening was going to be then? A strip-them-naked affair? An opportunity to out everyone from their protective shells and savage their soft inner parts? Or just an innocent hang out for old times' sake?

Ifeoma was asking herself the same question. Was it curiosity? A chance to talk over old times with the children now become women she had attended secondary school with? An opportunity to show off? Or just a little matter of seizing the occasion of Ife's daughter's wedding on Easter Monday to see what everyone was looking like and doing after so long? Unconsciously, she looked at her forearm. Tight muscles testified to her workout regime. Her biceps and triceps were good too. The only one of the girls she had met in all these years was Mildred. She hadn't even recognized some of the rest when they walked into the restaurant. This meeting had been arranged on their alumni platform.

"Where is the reception tomorrow?" It was Ebere, eyebrow arched in a characteristic manner. Ebere lived in Surrey with her husband, a medical doctor and their two perfect children.

How she had produced children who were academic award winners, Ifeoma couldn't imagine. She had been an average student back in the day. She was home for the Easter.

"Grand Multipurpose Center." Ebere acknowledged the answer from Cynthia with a nod.

And then there was Cynthia. That girl had been so promising in school, an A student all the way, but these days, she lived in one of the satellite cities with a husband who was a spare parts dealer. Mildred realized Cynthia hadn't said much all evening. Probably overwhelmed. Maureen said she owned a shop in the market near her

house, selling plastics. *Olisa ekwekwana!*
Mentally, Mildred circled her head
with her fingers and snapped them
away from her to ward off evil.
Choices. Mildred reflected on the
choices that turn people's destinies
on their heads. Cynthia had gotten
married right after school having
fallen pregnant for the spare
parts dealer. And now, she was
struggling to fit into this company.

Maureen made up the number. Hot
had always described her right from
their school days. She oozed a potent
sensuality that was as much part of her
as her signature braids. Maureen had
always been the one everyone thought

would lose it, speaking about her virginity, even before school wore out. Not dear Cynthia. Ironically, Cynthia who was the chapel prefect in those days, had filled that bill, and Maureen was these days, an international business woman with a loving husband and five children. She had just returned from Turkey on a shopping expedition for her boutique, and kept giving gentle tired yawns between conversation.

Bisi waved her fork for attention, "the church service is at ten in the morning right?" Everyone echoed "yes, ten," and she shook her head, full curly extensions bouncing around a face that looked thirty five instead of her real age of forty seven, and declared solemnly, "Then the best I can do is to aim for the reception. I don't think I will be done sleeping by even nine o clock *sef.*" Maureen concurred. "Don't expect me either. I have to catch up on some beauty sleep. *Man no be wood o!*"

The conversation became general again, until Ify brought it back to Hope. Hope was the icon of the Class of '83. For everyone at that table, she defined the success they had all dreamed about when they were young girls. Every woman at that table had hoped to get to the top of their careers, marry well, move in the right circles, make a name for themselves... Their headteacher had taught them ambition. Never to let their gender limit them, and anyone who was at this table this evening could see she had mentored them well.

Hope was the one who had it all. A career in the lucrative oil sector; serious connections across the country, and a husband who was also an oil mogul. She was on the society pages of all the weekend newspapers and the old girls followed her every move avidly. Cynthia, possibly more than all the rest, because in following Hope, she relived all her lost dreams.

Hope tried to open her eyes and focus. It was hard. Too hard. They kept sliding down by themselves like an automatic garage door. The young man touched her again, sensually, suggestively. She pressed against him and kissed him. Who was this person, she wondered, through the fog. Anyway whoever he was, he was nice and he was here. Ben was not. Ben was never around. Right now, he was away on a business trip to Brazil for two weeks even at this Easter season. Sometimes, when she was really lonely, like today, she pulled out all the stops.

She would take him to the guest house. Not to the house in Ikoyi. The management of the guest house were all her people, from her own village. She had personally interviewed, handpicked and paid each of them well and they were loyal to her alone. Inside that exquisite duplex, she lived her other life wrapped in their silence.

When the night stopped, Hope did not know. Her account rang all night with massive withdrawals and fell silent by morning. The guest house staff were used to young men leaving alone at dawn, and this was no different. Yesterday, they had barely looked at him, this morning, they looked even less, as he caught a taxi at the gate and went his way.

It was Easter Monday. The girls as

they still liked to call themselves woke up to the news, and began calling and chatting with each other for confirmation. As they filed into the Cathedral of St. John in their wedding best, they whispered among themselves. They would not tell Ife yet, they were fairly sure that with all the last minute stuff tied to weddings, she had probably not heard. How did you break this sort of news on a day like this?

Mildred looked at her bare arm. It was covered with goose pimples. What were the odds that this would be the breaking news today. Uncanny, terrible, timing.

"The body of top society socialite, Hope Ndigwe, was yesterday discovered in a Guest House belonging to the Ndigwe family at ... Suspected murder... An unidentified young man left the scene this morning... wife of oil magnate Ben Ndigwe...

Bisi who had changed her mind that morning about attending the church service saw the story scroll across the screen on the television in her hotel room, screamed "Jesus"! Reached for the remote control to turn up the volume, and immediately grabbed her phone to call Ibime.

The electronic shrill announced the news bite dropping into Ifeoma's phone as she dressed up for the wedding. She glanced at her phone, and nearly dropped it. Ify burst into sudden emotional tears, with one of her red shoes still clutched in her hand.

Mildred saw it through cascading thoughts and whispered to herself, "this life is deep." Nnamdi, her husband, fussing with his collar, turned and asked, "what did you say?"

"You won't understand. Today I realize that some things that glitter are not diamonds, they are broken glass."

HEALING

Like the fragrant perfume of a
sun-warmed garden, your love
envelopes me

Like the gentle touch of a skilled
physician, your love heals me

Like a plate of rich soup with assorted
meats and swallow, your love feeds
me

Like a gentle wind from heaven, your
love fans away the heat of my pain

And as I sit and soak you in, I know
beyond any doubt that I am beloved

———— **VICTIM** ————

I prayed until the floor around my knees was wet with tears. I prayed until I had no more strength to pray. My knees hurt. I sat down on the bare floor beside my bed, quieted my breathing, and let the wall clock tick away the seconds.

I think I must have slept because sometime toward morning I woke up with my head pillowed on my arms. I was startled awake, really. The dream had come again. I found myself on my back, inside in a room with red and black curtains, I lay in a huge bed covered with a red duvet. Suddenly, merciless hands forced my legs apart and there was a sharp pain. The blood gushed out with pumping force: a river of blood pouring out from inside me. A wet crimson tide soaking the duvet.

Twice in one night. I looked at the wall clock and it was five am in the morning. The same dream that had sent me to my knees crying for mercy had woken me up again. Twice in one night. I untangled my stiff limbs and limped over to the toilet. The dreams had become more frequent since Ifeanyi asked me to be his wife. Ifeanyi and I met in Apostolic Hope Church one sunny Saturday morning. When the taxi dropped me at the gate of the church, he was just arriving in his car, and he pulled over for me to get in. I wondered who he was, since I knew most people in church. I had never seen this face before. Sometimes I attended the two services, so it couldn't be because he was a ten am-er as we referred to those who preferred to attend the later service.

"Good morning," He smiled at the uncertain look on my face.

"Are you not going for choir practice? That's where I am headed for. This is my first day."

Ifeanyi, I found out, was an oil company engineer, who had just been moved from Port Harcourt to his head office in Abuja. He later told me he hadn't been too happy about leaving the bustling city of PH for the more laid back Abuja, but he had decided to make the best of it, first of all by finding a worship place and getting committed.

Conversation with him was easy.

"I joined Apostolic Hope last week. I was a chorister in my church in Port Harcourt, and I didn't want to stop serving Jesus because of this relocation."

I loved the way he spoke about his faith with comfortable ease. Ifeanyi was easy on the eye too. An open face with a dimple in the right cheek that was turned to me.

I remember wishing that the short drive to our second gate could have lasted longer, but we got there soon enough. Anyway since we were both in the same choir, we would probably see quite a bit of each other.

Months later, it was Nonso who gave me the first hint that my friendship with Ifeanyi could be headed somewhere more serious.

"Sister!" I turned to find Nonso grinning at me as I arrived early for choir practice that morning. I had gone over to the altar to pray before moving to the choir area. Nonso was not only our bass guitarist, but also one of three men in the choir who had asked me to pray and see what God would say about our getting married. When I told Nonso I did not receive a go ahead from heaven, he took it in good faith and we remained friends.

We were both quite early.

"You are looking good." I looked down at my print blue blouse over a long black skirt and said,

"Really? Thanks."

"But even if you wear sackcloth and ashes, there are people that I know who will still think you are the best thing since fried egg." He played a riff and I waited for him to tune his guitar; I knew he would say more. I wanted to hear more.

"Do you want to know who?"

"If you want to tell me, you will tell me. *No be you start the conversation?*" I reached for a hymn book in the stack nearby, pretending to be unconcerned.

"You know that me and Ifeanyi have become rather good friends *abi*? Anyway, he told me that he hopes your own friendship with him will become something more than that. I am sure he will tell you himself *sha*, so let me come and be minding my own business." He thrummed on his instrument a bit, and did some more tuning. Just then, Sandra and Afiniki came in and the conversation became general.

My pain went back fifteen years to the life I had before. A life that twisted me, and totally bent me out of shape.

"Okenna, do not go to bed until you finish washing those dirty pots. Do you hear me?"

My madam turned her ample body and entered the house. She let the net door to the kitchen slam behind her with an angry clap. I knew that today would be one of those days. Any time her menses were about to start, she would be like a mad woman picking quarrels with everyone around the house. Soon there would be bloody underwear to wash, but as disgusting as that was, it was still better than the screams and slaps that were part of this season in the Okoli household. Soon she stalked back into the kitchen.

"Who left those clothes that are already dry on the washing line?"

She stormed over to where I stood, anticipating the worst, with the metal sponge for scouring the pots gripped in my hand. She took hold of my left ear and gave it a vicious twist. Blinding pain erupted in my head. As I tried to move away, she twisted harder. I screamed with pain, and she pushed me hard against the sink and slammed out of the kitchen again. I sat down on the bare greasy cement floor of the kitchen, and let the tears soak my faded house dress, one of only three that I had. Alternately, I tried to nurse my burning ear and the pain in my side where I had hit the sink in falling.

I heard her coming again, quickly jumped up, pain forgotten, and began to scrub the pots as if my life depended on it. She looked in and uttered a long hiss like a spitting cobra. I could hear her walking away.

"*Anumani*! Animal. That is how you will go to the bush and get these dirty creatures, and when they come to your house, they will become bigger than you. Don't finish washing those pots. You will sleep inside the kitchen today."

That night, I finished my chores by eleven in the night, and went to my small room in the "Boy's Quarters" to sleep. It felt as if I had barely closed my eyes before heavy knocking on the door announced I was late to start another day.

My father lost his job as a messenger in a government office, and my mother was a petty trader selling soup ingredients in the local market. With seven children to feed, there was no way they could cope financially. The only solution my parents could think of was, "Let Okenna and Nkechi go out to live with other people. Maybe they will find their destiny there if God helps us." That was the sad decision.

The day Madam Okoli came for me, she was dressed in a pink and red print buba. Her smooth, round face had a pleasant smile pinned permanently to it. She handed over the envelope with my first salary inside it to my parents, and said, "we don't have much time. Let us be going. It will take us six hours to get there."

That is how we left the home in which I was born. My mother and my younger siblings were crying and clinging to me. I looked at the wooden doors and window shutters of our house in the village. I stared longingly at the orange and guava trees we used to climb to get sweet fruits in season. I even looked at our leaky zinc roof where rats would race each other noisily all night, and sniffed hard to keep back the tears. There was no help for it. Poverty parted us and I started my new life.

I got used to the slaps and knocks after a while, but nothing prepared me for the next level of torture I would endure in that home.

The first time it happened, I was twelve years old. My Madam had travelled to Aba to buy trade goods. I had settled the children for the night, taken my bath, and was lying in my small bed with a wrapper tied round my upper body because of the heat. It was about to rain.

When I saw the handle of my door turning, I was going to scream, and my heart nearly stopped beating. Thieves! How could I shout so that my master would hear, but they wouldn't. They were already at the door. Where could I hide in this tiny room?

The door opened and someone came in. Even through my terror, I knew from his body smell that it was my master, Mr. Okoli. He came straight to the bed where I was lying, covered my mouth with one hairy hand and tore off the wrapper with the other. I twisted and turned, bit his hand, tried to scream, but it was no good. As he tore into my body, I lost faith in life itself. It became a custom that whenever Madam travelled, her husband would sleep in my room. I took to praying that she would not travel.

I got pregnant when I was fourteen, and it was my madam who found out.

Her eyes filled with venom, she kept screaming and slapping me.

"Whore! *Na who give you de belle? Ashawo! As small as you are you already know man!* Tell me, or I will kill you today!"

To stop the beating, I told her I would tell her in my room. She dragged me there.

"*Oya tell me! Tell me!* Who did you open your legs for?"

"It is your husband," I told her quietly. "Any time you travel, he will come and force me."

She screamed,

"*You are a liar! Anu ofia!*"

But she could see the truth in my face, and I could see the truth in her eyes. She sat down on my small bed, her fat body deflating like a balloon punctured with a pin.

Suddenly, she jumped up, rushed into the house, and I could hear her shouting, "Papa Ebenezer, you will kill me today, and if you make the mistake of not killing me, I will kill you! This is what you did to the last girl I brought to this house. So you have done it again?"

Sounds of blows and trampling filled the whole house. The noise of things crashing and breaking. After some time, she returned to my room with a fresh bruise on her forehead. "Put on your dress and follow me."

The private hospital we went to seemed to know her well. When she left the waiting room to see the doctor inside, the matron hissed, "Witch! The judgment of God will surely fall on her. That is how she keeps bringing little children here to destroy their lives." I shivered.

The abortion did not take long. No one prepared me for the pain. Not only the pain inside my body, but the scraping pain in my soul. When we returned to that house, I decided I would not stay any more.

Pastor Ndukanma adopted me after

I told him and his wife my story. They had a church near to the Okolis, and lived in the church premises. Over the years, they had seen and heard what I was going through. It was to their house I ran as soon I was strong enough, and told them my whole story.

When my parents heard from them, they agreed to allow me to live with them as their child. I grew up in their house as a cherished daughter, and it was his wife who led me to Christ.

The day Ifeanyi asked me to marry him, I was not surprised. I knew it was coming, but I also knew what my answer would be.

"I can't."

"You can't? Why? Don't you feel anything for me?"

"I do, but I can't."

He looked at me puzzled, struggling to understand. I told him part of the story. I came from a poor family. I wasn't born to privilege. In fact in my early life, I had been a house help. Did he want to marry a house help?" Ifeanyi looked relieved. "Is that all? Are house helps not human beings? Do you know whether I used to be a house boy?"

I couldn't help smiling.

"Nana, I won't accept that answer. Go and pray and see what God will tell you."

After that, the dreams began to come. Nothing seemed to stop them. Not prayer, not fasting, nothing. I shared with my prayer partner Afiniki.

"My sister, there is something you don't know about me."

She turned her eyes to me, waiting.

"When I was twelve, the man whose wife brought me to Lagos began to rape me. When I was fourteen, I got pregnant."

I could see the pity in her eyes as she waited.

"My Madam took me to the hospital and the pregnancy was aborted."

"Yesu!"

The cry was involuntary. Afiniki moved over and put her arm around my shoulder trying to draw out my pain. She was speaking in tongues.

"Almost every night, I dream about the abortion. I want to tell Ifeanyi. I don't even know if I can still have children."

She stared at me, cutting off her prayers. "Why would you want to do that? Don't. What if he says he is no longer interested?"

I wrestled with my soul for one more week, then I told Ifeanyi.

"Is that what you tried to tell me the other day?"

Silence. I stared at the floor, lost in my pain.

"Nne, even if you told me you cut off someone's head sometime in your past life, I would still marry you. Old things have passed away. You were the victim, not the offender. Do you understand?" He gently placed a hand on my shoulder.

Fifteen years of subliminal fear began to melt away under that touch. For what felt like the first time in years not days, I lifted my face and smiled.

— ODE TO THE AFRICAN —
WOMAN

You are a voluptuous mystery
With a deep and ancient history
Your contours have
embraced humanity
Your beauty has defied mastery

You are owned by none, yet
 owned by all
Breasts and shoulders erect, you
walk tall
Bearing heavy burdens to a distant
market stall

Determined, hunger and penury
to forestall

Your eyes have seen a thousand wars
Your body has borne the trail of a
hundred paws
Yet power and dignity ooze from your
very pores
Heart never questioning what
it endures

Woman of great beauty
Sister of honour and nobility

You have no voice to speak of your
own
So, today for you I must speak to atone
for years of silence, as you sat alone,
bearing life with a smile on a face like
stone